# GROWING UP *with* UP
# Autism

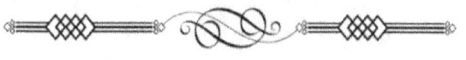

ROBERT LEE DOCKERY

ASA PUBLISHING CORPORATION
AN INNOVATIVE OUTSOURCE BOOK PUBLISHING HYBRID

ASA Publishing Corporation
1285 N. Telegraph Rd. PMB #351,
Monroe, Michigan 48162
*An Accredited Publishing House with the BBB*

## www.asapublishingcorporation.com

Copyrights©2025, Robert Lee Dockery, All Rights Reserved
Book Title: Growing Up with Autism
Date Published: 03.24.2025
Book ID: ASAPCID2380941
Edition: 1 *Trade Paperback*
ISBN: 978-1-960104-75-5
Library of Congress Cataloging-in-Publication Data

This book was published in the United States of America.
Great State of Michigan

## Introduction:

## A Journey of Resilience and Triumph

Life is not defined by the challenges we face, but by how we rise above them. Hi, my name is PJ Brown, the one in the center, and my story is one of determination, resilience, and triumph against the odds. Born in 1975 in Brooklyn, New York, I was diagnosed with autism at the age of two—a condition that was widely misunderstood at the time. Growing up in the vibrant yet harsh streets of New York, I faced challenges that tested my spirit. From navigating developmental delays to enduring bullying and witnessing the devastating effects of the crack epidemic, I encountered a world that wasn't always kind or accommodating.

But my journey wasn't just about obstacles—it was also filled with unwavering love and support from my family, teachers, and friends. My mother's boundless determination and belief in my potential shaped me into the person I am today. Alongside her, individuals like my cousin Mark, who's on my right, my teachers, and my close friends played pivotal roles in helping me discover my voice, my passions, and ultimately, my path.

Basketball became my sanctuary, a place where I could rise above adversity and prove that I was more than my diagnosis. From humble beginnings at the milk-crate-rimmed courts of New York to the bright lights of the NBA, I defied expectations and made history as the first autistic basketball player in the league. Along the way, I forged lifelong friendships, inspired others, and left an indelible mark on the world of sports.

My story is not just about my journey; it's about the message I carry for others: that no matter where you come from or what challenges you face, your dreams are valid, and your potential is limitless. This is a story of resilience, community, and the power of never giving up—a story that I hope will inspire others to pursue their dreams and embrace the unique brilliance within themselves.

# GROWING UP *with* Autism

# Chapter one

My name is PJ Brown, and I was born in 1975 in Brooklyn, New York. Life had barely begun for me when, at the age of two, I was diagnosed with autism—a condition that, in those days, carried little understanding and even fewer resources. But if there's one thing my mother, Kandi, taught me, it's that love and determination can move mountains.

From the start, my mom noticed that I wasn't like the other toddlers in our neighborhood. While they babbled, toddled, and explored, I remained in my own world—silent, still crawling, and lagging far behind in my developmental milestones. My mom, ever the fighter, refused to accept uncertainty when it came to me. Her worry was tangible, as was her hope. She knew something wasn't right, but she also believed in finding a way forward.

One day, driven by her growing concerns, my mom took me to see Dr. John, a soft-spoken pediatrician whose calm demeanor made her feel, even if just for a moment, less alone. As she explained my struggles—how I wasn't talking, how my frustration turned into overwhelming tantrums, how I flapped my hands and stared off into space— her voice trembled with both fear and resolve. Dr. John listened carefully, reassuring her with the words she so desperately needed to hear: "We'll figure this out."

Tests were run. My hearing was fine, but when Dr. John tried to engage me in speech exercises, I simply crawled away, my little hands flapping as if propelled by an internal rhythm only I could understand. It was then, after observing these signs, that Dr. John gave my mother the news: I was on the autism spectrum. In that moment, the weight of the world seemed to rest on my mother's shoulders.

"What can I do to help my son?" she pleaded, tears brimming in her eyes. Dr. John, recognizing her unwavering determination, told her about Grant Preschool, a place equipped to support autistic children like me. "You're blessed to have found me," he added gently. "Autism isn't well-known yet, but I understand it, and the people at Grant do too. They'll help guide you through this journey."

My mom's gratitude was boundless. She hugged Dr. John and whispered, "Thank you for giving me hope." As we left that day, her spirit, though heavy with responsibility, was also infused with newfound purpose.

When the fall of 1977 arrived, so did my first day at Grant Preschool. My mom held my hand tightly as we walked into the cheerful building, where we were greeted by Mrs. Ross, a warm and compassionate teacher whose smile seemed to light up the room. My mother's voice quivered as she explained my diagnosis, her vulnerability laid bare. But Mrs. Ross, like Dr. John, offered comfort and reassurance. "We'll help your son," she promised. "You're in the right place."

That day marked the beginning of a new chapter for both of us. At home, life remained a struggle. My tantrums were loud, heartbreaking expressions of my frustration. I'd scream, bang my head against walls, and thrash in my highchair. My mom did everything she could to calm me— offering snacks, apple juice, and above all, her love. Watching me suffer was agonizing for her, but she never let her exhaustion show. She was my constant, my anchor, and my fiercest advocate.

When she had to work as a maid, my cousin Mark stepped in to care for me. Mark, tall, strong, and endlessly patient, filled the room with laughter and energy. He'd read me stories, chase me around the house in games of tag, and find ways to bring joy into my silent world. On my first day at Grant, it was Mark who held my hand as I walked into the classroom and met Mrs. Ross. "We'll do everything we can for him," she promised Mark, and for the first time, I felt surrounded by people determined to see me thrive.

In class, I met Bradley, a five-year-old autistic boy with a remarkable memory and a gift for connecting with others. Though I wasn't speaking yet, Bradley made sure I felt included. He encouraged me to count on my fingers and interact with our classmates. Small victories, like pointing at pictures to choose my lunch, were met with smiles and praise. These moments, though modest, were monumental to my mom—they were signs of progress, of hope, and of a brighter future.

The day I finally spoke my first word was nothing short of magical—both for me and my mom. It began with a simple yet life-changing moment. I said, "Mama." At first, it felt strange to form the sound, as if my voice was unlocking a long-hidden door. But once that door opened, the words started tumbling out. I walked into the house, my heart pounding with excitement, and shouted in a high-pitched voice, "Mama!"

My mom came rushing downstairs, her face a mix of shock and joy. When she saw me standing there, her eyes filled with tears. For years, she had prayed and hoped for this moment—to hear my voice. And now, here it was, clear and undeniable. "Mama, I love you," I said, my small voice cracking with the unfamiliarity of speaking. My mom dropped to her knees and held me close, her tears falling freely. "I love you too, PJ," she whispered, her voice trembling with overwhelming emotion.

Overcome with happiness, my mom ran outside to find Bradley, who was playing on the sidewalk.

"Bradley!" she called out, "How is my son talking? I can't believe it!"

Bradley, ever modest, smiled and said, "I've been practicing with my good friend PJ ever since he was little, Mrs. Brown."

My mom hugged him tightly, tears still streaming down her face. "God bless you, Bradley," she said. "You've truly helped my son in ways I can never repay. I'm going to tell his teachers—everyone has to know he can talk now!"

Bradley had always been a quiet but steady presence in my life, guiding me with patience and care. He would encourage me to say words, working alongside Mrs. Hanson, another dedicated teacher, to help me find my voice. The teachers admired Bradley's kindness and intelligence, often praising him for assisting not just me but other autistic kids in our class.

That evening, my cousin Mark came over. The moment he walked through the door, I greeted him with, "What's up, cousin?" Mark froze, stunned by the words he had just heard. Slowly, a grin spread across his face, and he pulled me into a giant bear hug. "I can't believe it, PJ," he said, his voice filled with pride. For Mark, this moment was just as surreal as it had been for my mom. He had been there for me through the toughest times, supporting me with unwavering devotion. Hearing me speak felt like a weight had been lifted—a shared burden we'd been carrying together for years.

By 1981, I was finally speaking clearly and fluently. It wasn't just a milestone for me—it was a victory for everyone who had been by my side on this journey. My family's pride in me was immeasurable, and their belief in my potential never wavered. Looking back, I realize that their love and support were the foundation of every step forward I took. Their patience, persistence, and hope had carried me through, and now, for the first time, I could finally say the words they had waited so long to hear.

# Chapter two

In the fall of 1981, I started elementary school at Teddy Elementary as a kindergartener. I was six years old, a year older than most of my classmates, but I didn't feel ashamed. I knew my journey with autism had been different, and I refused to let it define me. My teacher, Mrs. Banks, was a tall, blonde woman in her 30s with a no-nonsense demeanor. On the first day, she greeted us warmly, saying, "Welcome to Teddy Elementary! Are you ready to get to know each other and me?" We all nodded eagerly.

Mrs. Banks introduced an icebreaker game where we'd share something about ourselves. When it was my turn, she smiled and said, "PJ, tell us a little about yourself."

I stood up, my heart pounding, and said, "My favorite colors are red, white, and blue, and I love reading books."

Mrs. Banks beamed. "That's wonderful, PJ! I love books too. I bet some of your classmates do as well."

She encouraged me to share more, so I added, "I also love playing arcade games like Pac-Man and Galaga. I'm really good at them—it's my special talent."

My classmates were amazed, especially a girl named Kayla, who challenged me to a game of Pac-Man. "We can go to the arcade after school," I said confidently.

Kayla grinned. "I'll have to ask my mom first, but I want to see if you're as good as you say you are."

I smiled back. "Trust me, I am."

After introductions, we headed outside for recess. Socializing in large groups was always a challenge for me, but I found comfort in smaller circles. I spent recess swinging on the swings with my friends Michael, Kayla, Johnny, and Bradley. We had swinging contests, and I often won, soaring higher than anyone else. Kayla was my closest competitor, always finishing second. We also climbed the monkey bars, though I struggled to hold on for long because my hands would hurt.

Back in class, Mrs. Banks laid out her rules: respect each other and treat others the way you want to be treated. She was strict, and as an autistic child, her criticism often stung. When she pointed out that I was slow at certain tasks, I'd feel a lump in my throat and tears welling up. But I tried my best to improve, even when it was hard.

After school, I approached Kayla. "Do you still want to play Pac-Man?" I asked.

She nodded. "Let me ask my mom first. You can come over to my house."

My mom didn't mind me hanging out with friends—she encouraged it—but she always reminded me to be home before the streetlights came on.

Kayla's house was big like mine, though less decorated. After getting her mom's permission, we headed to the arcade. The moment we walked in, I was mesmerized by the rows of games: Galaga, Pac-Man, Donkey Kong, Popeye, and later, Street Fighter. The arcade, called Chinatown Fair, was a bustling hub where kids gathered after school. I was one of the best players, with my wins and losses tallied on a whiteboard. My name was consistently at the top.

Kayla and I started our Pac-Man match. I went first, maneuvering Pac-Man with precision, tricking the ghosts, and clearing level after level. When I hit a high score of 100,000, Kayla finally looked impressed. "Wow, PJ, I didn't know you were this good!" she said. "I usually beat my friends, but you're on another level." Kayla took her turn, reaching 70,000 before losing. "You're amazing, PJ," she admitted. "I see now why this is your special talent." Later, we went back to my house, where my mom was chatting with Mrs. Ross on the couch.

"Hi, Mom," I said. "Kayla and I had fun at the arcade, and I beat her in Pac-Man."

My mom smiled proudly. "That's wonderful, PJ. Mrs. Ross and I were just talking about how much progress you've made this year. We're so proud of you."

During my time at Teddy Elementary (1981–1985), I made significant strides. I excelled in math, quickly mastering addition and subtraction, and my reading skills were advanced for my age. Mrs. Banks often asked me to read to the class, and I enjoyed it, earning admiration from my classmates. However, handwriting was a struggle, and Mrs. Banks frequently reminded me to practice. "You need to work on this, PJ," she'd say, and I'd promise to try harder.

Not everything was smooth sailing. I faced bullying from Russo, a heavyset boy with a reputation for trouble, and his sidekicks, Billy and

Pete. They targeted me and my friends, often locking kids in lockers or mocking autistic students. I stood up to them, but the fights were unfair—three against one. One day, they threw batteries at me, breaking my nose. When I got home, my mom was furious.

"Those boys have been picking on you again?" she asked.

I nodded. "Yes, but I stood up for myself."

My mom called my cousin Mark, who arrived in his 1983 Corvette, ready to take action.

Mark and I went to the school, but Russo and his gang weren't there. We found them at the Chinatown Fair arcade. Mark confronted Russo, and a fight broke out. I joined in, swinging at Billy, while Michael, another classmate who had also been bullied, stepped in to help. Together, we stood up to the bullies, showing them that we wouldn't back down.

The fight at the arcade was chaotic and intense, a whirlwind of emotions and actions that I'll never forget. Mark, my cousin, had blackened

Russo's eye, but Russo retaliated, tackling Mark to the ground with the force of his massive, sumo-like frame. Just as it seemed Mark was pinned, Michael, my classmate and friend, stepped in. He grabbed a heavy glass bottle and struck Russo on the head. The sound of the impact echoed through the arcade, and Russo collapsed, bleeding and motionless, his large body sprawled on the floor.

Meanwhile, I was locked in my own battle with Billy. Fueled by years of frustration and a newfound determination, I picked him up and slammed him to the ground. I climbed on top of him, punching his face until it was bloody. When I finally stood up, I stomped on his face—a moment that filled me with a mix of pride and disbelief. For the first time, I had stood up to the bullies who had tormented me, and I felt a surge of empowerment.

The chaos didn't go unnoticed. Police officers stormed into the arcade, shouting for everyone to leave. We scrambled to get out, but they caught Michael still fighting Pete and arrested him on the spot. As Michael was led away in handcuffs, the police cordoned off the area with yellow tape, turning the arcade into a crime scene. The ambulance arrived shortly after, attempting to save Russo, but his injuries were severe. The paramedics worked quickly, but the open wound on his head revealed the extent of the damage—blood and brain tissue were visible. Despite their efforts, Russo was pronounced dead at the hospital.

The news of Russo's death hit me hard. I felt a pang of guilt for what had happened, even though I hadn't been the one to deliver the fatal blow. Michael, who had only been trying to protect me, now faced the possibility of being tried as an adult for murder. The weight of it all was overwhelming.

When I got home, Mark dropped me off before heading to the gym to work out. During the car ride, he expressed his pride in me for standing up to the bullies. "You did good, PJ," he said, his voice filled with admiration. Later, he called my mom to recount the events, and when she came home, she wrapped me in a hug so tight it felt like being embraced by a bear. "I'm so proud of you, PJ," she said, her voice thick with emotion. "You stood up for yourself like a big boy."

That evening, as I sat on the porch, I saw a figure walking down the street—a frail, older woman who looked eerily familiar. I ran inside to tell my mom, and when she came out to see, her face froze in shock.

"PJ, that's your speech teacher, Mrs. Hanson," she said, her voice heavy with disbelief. "I think she's strung out on crack."

Confused, I asked, "What's crack, Mom?"

She explained, "It's a dangerous drug that's destroying lives here in New York. Promise me you'll never touch it, PJ."

I nodded, but my heart sank.

Seeing Mrs. Hanson, the woman who had once guided me with patience and care, now reduced to this state, was devastating. The crack epidemic was ravaging our community, and witnessing its impact firsthand was a harsh reality I struggled to process.

Mrs. Hanson's decline weighed on me. She would approach me on the street, her movements erratic, asking if I had a "rock." Each encounter was a painful reminder of how far she had fallen. The woman who had once been a pillar of support in my life was now a shadow of her former self, and it broke my heart.

Seeking solace, I went inside to practice my handwriting. As I wrote, I noticed something remarkable—my handwriting had suddenly become neater, more legible. My mom walked in and saw my work. Her face lit up with pride. "I just thank God y'all didn't get caught by the police at that arcade," she said, relief evident in her voice. "Lord knows I would've had a fit if something happened to y'all."

I told her how Mark had driven us away so fast it nearly gave me a heart attack. She laughed, her tension easing for a moment. Then she looked at my paper and said, "PJ, your handwriting is beautiful now. It's all coming together for you." Her words filled me with a sense of accomplishment.

Despite the challenges I faced, I was making progress—progress that felt monumental in a time when autism was so poorly understood.

My mom often reminded me how blessed we were to have found Dr. John, the doctor who had first diagnosed me. "He really helped us, PJ," she said. "And look at you now—you're overcoming so much." Her pride and unwavering support were the foundation of my strength, and I carried her words with me as I continued to navigate the complexities of life.

# Chapter three

I attended Danson Middle School from 1987 to 1988, a time that brought both challenges and heartbreak. Early in the school year, I learned that my friend Michael had been sentenced to life in prison for the fight at the arcade. The news devastated me. Michael had only been trying to defend himself and his friends, yet the system treated him as an adult, stripping away his future. I saw him on the news, sitting in the courtroom, and my heart sank. My mom, watching with me, said, "Thank God you and Mark didn't get caught." I nodded, relieved that the police hadn't come knocking on our door, but the weight of Michael's fate lingered heavily.

Later that day, Mark came over and saw Michael's trial on TV. "How did this happen?" he asked, his voice filled with disbelief. I explained that Michael had been arrested on the scene for fighting Pete. Mark shook his head. "Damn, man. That sucks. I hope he has a good lawyer." His words echoed my own thoughts—Michael deserved better.

At school, my teacher, Mr. Briggs, greeted me with his usual energy. "What's up? What's your name?" he asked. "PJ," I replied. Mr. Briggs was a hyperactive man, always moving, always loud. He had a habit of yelling at students when they struggled, so I quickly learned to figure things out on my own. One day, during class, he abruptly ran out to address a commotion in the neighboring room, which housed the mentally impaired students. "See you, bye," he said, leaving us behind.

The incident next door involved Corey, a non-verbal autistic student who was having a meltdown. Other kids had been bullying him, leaving scratches on his face and a black eye. Mr. Lance, the teacher in the mentally impaired room, tried his best to manage the chaos. Corey's parents didn't answer the phone, and while Mr. Lance was trying to call them again, another student attempted to climb out of the window. Mr. Lance, a kind and patient man, managed to pull the student back to safety, but the stress of handling so many students alone was evident.

Despite the challenges, Mr. Lance's methods were ahead of their time. He treated his students with respect and encouraged them to try new things while allowing them to feel comfortable in their own ways. His dedication stood in stark contrast to Mr. Mosley, a teacher who was rarely present because he was addicted to crack. Mr. Mosley's absence left Mr. Lance to shoulder the burden alone, yet he persevered with remarkable compassion.

Back in my classroom, Mr. Briggs returned and resumed teaching Algebra. I couldn't believe we were tackling algebra on the first day of school, but I was determined to succeed. At first, I struggled with the assignment, but I eventually figured it out. When I turned in my work, Mr. Briggs was impressed. "Wow, PJ, I'm going to show this to the class," he said. At that moment, I felt a surge of pride—I had proven to myself that I could rise to the challenge.

After school, I walked home and noticed an unsettling change in my neighborhood. The crack epidemic had transformed our once-quiet streets into a dangerous place. Crackheads loitered on corners, and gunshots echoed through the night, making it hard to sleep. My mom taught me to always watch my back, a lesson I took to heart as I navigated the chaos.

One day, while walking to school, I met David, a cool and laid-back guy with short dreads and a big smile. We bonded instantly over our shared love of arcade games like Pac-Man and

Street Fighter. David and I became fast friends, excelling as partners on school projects and earning top grades together.

But the crack epidemic's reach was inescapable. One morning, as David and I walked to school, we encountered Mrs. Banks, my former teacher from Teddy Elementary. She was unrecognizable, strung out on crack.

She approached us, asking, "Do you have a rock?"

David, disgusted, yelled, "Hell no! Get away from us!"

I told him, "She used to be my teacher."

David shook his head. "Man, crack is the devil. It's destroying everyone."

The epidemic's impact extended to my school. One day, Mr. Briggs, who had been unusually hyperactive, suddenly collapsed in class. Mr. Lance rushed in to help, performing CPR until the ambulance arrived. Despite their efforts, Mr. Briggs didn't survive. The police later confirmed that he had overdosed on crack. The principal announced over the intercom that the school would be temporarily closed to investigate how drugs were infiltrating the campus. While the closure gave us a break from school, it was a stark reminder of the crisis consuming our community.

At home, my mom showed me one of the anti-drug commercials airing on TV. "PJ, promise me you'll never touch drugs," she said, her voice firm but loving. "I want you to be healthy and strong." Her words stayed with me, a guiding principle that kept me away from the temptations that claimed so many lives around me.

During middle school, I had a close-knit group of friends: David, CJ, Lewis, and Jr. We each had our quirks and talents, but together we were inseparable. Lewis was a skinny guy who always wore skinny jeans, a laid-back type who effortlessly went along with the flow. He lived around the corner from me, so we'd often hang out, spending hours at Chinatown Fair playing arcade games. Lewis admired my skills at the arcade, constantly amazed by how I dominated games like Pac-Man and Galaga.

"PJ, you should be a gamer," he'd say, impressed by my moves.

But I had different dreams. "I want to be a basketball player," I'd reply. "Like Patrick Ewing."

Lewis laughed, intrigued by my passion. "Okay, let's see what you've got," he said.

After one particularly competitive arcade session, we headed to his backyard to shoot some hoops. When I saw his setup—a basketball pole with a crate nailed on top instead of a traditional hoop—I paused, puzzled.

"Why do you shoot the basketball inside of a crate?" I asked.

Lewis grinned. "This is how we play basketball in the hood in New York," he explained.

I shrugged, eager to join in. Lewis took the ball first, dribbling with determination, but when it was my turn, I took control of the game. I dominated down low with my size advantage, shooting skyhooks over him with ease. Lewis, despite his agility, couldn't stop me from sinking shot after shot. "Man, you're unstoppable!" he said, shaking his head in mock defeat. I couldn't help but smile, feeling a surge of confidence. Basketball wasn't just a game—it was a glimpse into the dream I was chasing.

# Chapter four

I attended Sunny High School in the 1990s, and this is where my love for basketball truly blossomed. On the court, I found a space where I could thrive and showcase my talents. I developed a sharp three-point shot and a strong inside game that left my opponents struggling to keep up. My coach saw something special in me, often saying, "PJ, your game is ahead of its time. You're going to make the NBA one day." His words fueled my confidence and solidified my dreams of playing professionally.

Scouts started coming to my games, drawn by my skill and determination. Watching them scribble notes on clipboards as I played felt surreal—it was proof that my hard work was paying off. By the end of high school, I earned a scholarship to play basketball at Michigan. The moment I received the offer, I was overwhelmed with excitement. College was the next step toward my dream, and my mom couldn't have been prouder. She hugged me tightly, tears of joy streaming down her face, and said, "PJ, you've overcome so much to get here. I always knew you could do it."

As I transitioned to college basketball, my game continued to improve. My defense became a key strength, and my offensive skills grew more refined. It was here that I met Chris, a fellow basketball lover who quickly became my best friend. Chris and I were inseparable, sharing our love for the game and supporting each other both on and off the court. We played basketball, talked to girls, watched movies, played video games, and shared countless meals together. Chris had a natural charm with women, but he also excelled academically, earning top grades while maintaining his focus on basketball. He was a tall, light-skinned man with a confident, approachable demeanor that made him easy to connect with.

Our bond extended to teamwork in the classroom, where we tackled projects and assignments with precision. Teachers often praised us for our collaboration and the quality of our work, which only strengthened our friendship. Chris had my back in every sense of the word, and I knew I could always count on him.

During my time at Michigan, I also developed a deep relationship with Gina, a kind and thoughtful woman who became my anchor during challenging times. Gina and I clicked instantly, discovering shared passions and values that formed the foundation of our connection. She offered me a shoulder to lean on when I struggled and guided me with advice on how to improve my basketball game. Her positivity lifted me whenever I felt overwhelmed, and her presence brought a light into my life that I hadn't experienced before.

We spent hours walking together off-campus, talking about our dreams and finding solace in each other's company. Our chemistry didn't go unnoticed—people often commented on how we were the "cutest couple." Gina believed in me wholeheartedly. When I considered staying in college for another year, she urged me to declare for the NBA Draft and convinced me that I had the talent to excel immediately.

Her unwavering faith in me tipped the scales, and with her encouragement, I made the decision to enter the draft.

I graduated with a 3.5 GPA, earning the respect of my teachers, who also supported my decision to pursue the NBA.

In 1997, I was selected by the Sacramento Kings as the 35th overall pick in the NBA Draft. Hearing my name called was a moment of pure joy and triumph. My family erupted in celebration, and my mom hugged me tightly, her happy tears streaming down her cheeks. "PJ, you've made history," she said. "You're the first autistic basketball player to make it to the NBA, and I couldn't be prouder."

The draft experts praised the Kings for choosing me, recognizing the dedication and resilience that brought me to this moment.

One of them approached me and asked, "How does it feel to make your dream come true?"

I replied, "It feels incredible. I've come a long way—from struggling to talk as a child to now playing in the NBA alongside the greats. Growing up in a tough New York neighborhood and seeing my teachers succumb to drugs, I've faced so many challenges. But now, I'm here, ready to take on this new chapter."

The expert smiled and said, "You deserve this, PJ. Keep striving for greatness."

Gina shared in my excitement, kissing me on the cheek as we celebrated. But my mom quickly intervened, joking, "No grandbabies yet, you hear me?"

My NBA journey began with the summer

league, where I showcased my talents alongside other rookies. My lockdown defense and sharp shooting from the three-point line impressed coaches and NBA legends alike. Their predictions of my potential to have a Hall of Fame career pushed me to keep improving. My inside game was just as strong—I consistently dominated down low, earning respect and admiration from my fellow rookies.

Though I didn't play much during my rookie season, when I did step onto the court, I made an impact. My teammates appreciated my skills, and I felt confident in my abilities to contribute to the team. This was just the beginning of my dream—a dream built on hard work, resilience, and the unwavering support of the people who believed in me.

# Chapter five

My official welcome to the NBA moment came when Patrick Ewing, my childhood role model, dunked on me during a game. I was furious, but at the same time, I couldn't believe it had happened. It was a surreal reminder that I was sharing the court with legends—the same players I grew up idolizing. That moment was a reality check, solidifying in my mind that I had truly made it to the NBA.

By my second season, I had earned a spot in the starting lineup, thanks to head coach Rick Adelman's trust in my abilities. He wanted to see what I could do, and I didn't disappoint. I averaged an impressive 20 points per game, drawing praise from both my coach and my teammates. My work ethic became the talk of the locker room—I'd show up to practice early and leave late, perfecting my jump shots and pushing myself to new heights. The grueling intensity of NBA practices tested me, but I embraced the challenge. Each session helped me grow—not just as a player, but as a person, making me more resilient and disciplined.

I played a pivotal role in leading the Sacramento Kings to the playoffs that year, often stepping up in clutch moments and delivering on both ends of the court. My defense was sharp, and I relished the opportunity to guard some of the league's best players. The playoffs were exhilarating, even though we eventually fell to the Utah Jazz after holding a 2-1 series lead. I gave everything I had in that series, hitting tough shots and holding my ground defensively. John Stockton and Karl Malone, two of the greatest players of all time, went out of their way to praise my performance, and hearing their respect was an incredible validation of my progress.

Off the court, I forged deep friendships with teammates Chris Webber and Peja Stojaković. Our bond extended beyond basketball—we spent countless evenings bowling, where Peja often came out on top. While they enjoyed flirting with the girls at the bowling alley, I stayed faithful to Gina, the love of my life. The girls would ask for my autograph, and I'd happily oblige, also taking time to sign for kids and pose for pictures. After bowling, we'd head to my house, fire up my PS1, and stay up all night playing video games, laughing, and creating unforgettable memories.

The next morning, we'd treat ourselves to breakfast at some of California's finest restaurants—French toast was a favorite. Giving back to the community was also important to us, so we often spent time handing out food to those in need. It felt good to make a difference.

When I received my first NBA paycheck, I fulfilled one of my biggest dreams: moving my family out of New York. I bought my mom a beautiful mansion in Tampa, where she could finally sleep peacefully, far away from the dangers of our old neighborhood. I also got my cousin Mark a stunning house in Houston. Providing them with safety and comfort was one of my proudest achievements, and I felt an overwhelming sense of gratitude for everything they had done to support me.

In my third season, I truly came into my own, becoming one of the best two-way players in the league. My scoring average skyrocketed to 27 points per game, and my defense was at an elite level. I was named to my first All-Star game and played my heart out, hitting clutch shots and helping my team secure a victory. The recognition from players like Tim Duncan and Allen Iverson, who suggested I join their teams, made me feel like I had earned a place in the NBA family. Their respect was a reminder of how far I had come.

As the face of the Sacramento Kings, I led the team to the playoffs once again. We faced the Lakers in the first round, and while I played excellent defense on Kobe Bryant, his tough shots and the Lakers' prowess ultimately led to our defeat. Despite the loss, I was proud of how much I had grown as a player and the respect I had gained around the league.

By my fourth season, the Kings had transformed into an elite team, thanks in part to the chemistry I shared with Chris Webber and Peja Stojaković. Together, we struck fear into opponents as a formidable trio. We had a strong season, finishing with a 55-27 record and finally breaking through the first round by defeating the Phoenix Suns. Advancing felt like a huge weight had been lifted off our shoulders, though we were ultimately swept by the Lakers in the conference semifinals. Still, our progress signaled that we were now one of the league's best teams.

In my fifth season, I continued to elevate my game, earning my second consecutive All-Star appearance. Chris Webber missed some games due to injury, but the team rallied, proving our resilience by securing one of the best records in the NBA. Our deep playoff run included thrilling victories over the Utah Jazz and Dallas Mavericks, leading to my first-ever appearance in the Western Conference Finals. I was nervous, knowing how much was at stake, but Coach Adelman calmed my nerves, reminding me to focus on my game and not strive for perfection.

We faced the Lakers in a grueling series that pushed us to the brink. Holding a 3-2 lead, we were on the cusp of the NBA Finals, but Shaq's dominance in the paint and a series of controversial calls tilted the tide in their favor. The Lakers ultimately won in Game 7, and my heart broke. Watching them celebrate the championship was agonizing—I felt we had been robbed of our rightful shot at the title.

Tragedy struck in my sixth season when I tore my ACL, ending my basketball career. The news was devastating. Basketball had been my life, a source of joy, growth, and connection. Losing it felt like losing a part of myself. But as I processed the emotions—anger, sadness, and grief—I also found a sense of purpose. I knew this was my opportunity to pursue a new path. My teammates rallied around me, offering hugs and words of encouragement that reminded me I was not alone.

# Chapter six

After my basketball playing career came to an end, I transitioned into a new chapter of my life by working as an analyst for TNT and ESPN. Breaking down the game I loved and sharing insights with fans brought me a deep sense of satisfaction, but it wasn't my only focus. I also dedicated myself to charity work, specifically supporting autistic children. Giving back to the autistic community became a personal mission for me. I wanted to inspire others to chase their dreams, regardless of the challenges they faced. I wanted them to see that autism wasn't a limitation—it was a different way of viewing and navigating the world.

Part of my mission involved speaking at

schools to educate students and teachers about autism. I felt it was crucial to spread awareness and foster acceptance for people with disabilities. My message was clear: autism isn't a tragedy; it's simply a different way of experiencing and learning about the world. I emphasized that everyone has their own unique way of doing things, and those differences should be celebrated, not stigmatized.

In addition to my advocacy work, I stayed close to the game of basketball by training current NBA players during the off-season. Johnson Tatum, Luka Dončić, Donovan Mitchell, Kevin Durant, Trae Young, and many others sought my guidance. Watching them soak up knowledge like sponges and refine their games brought me immense joy. I shared not only the technical skills I had honed over my career but also the lessons I'd learned from growing up in New York and thriving in the NBA despite the challenges of autism. My story seemed to resonate with them, often leaving them inspired by the resilience and perseverance that had carried me through my journey.

Reflecting on my playing career, I felt an overwhelming sense of pride. Being the first autistic basketball player in the NBA was a groundbreaking achievement, and I was proud to have escaped the tough streets of New York to make my mark on the world.

My message to all autistic individuals is this: your dreams are within reach, no matter the obstacles. Disability does not define you, and you are capable of achieving greatness.